For Jonathan and Angela for
teaching me winning ways.
~DB

For Andrew, Robert and Elizabeth. x
~MS

LITTLE TIGER PRESS
An imprint of Magi Publications, 1 The Coda Centre,
189 Munster Road, London SW6 6AW, UK
www.littletigerpress.com
First published in Great Britain 2002
First American edition published 2003
This edition published 2010
Text copyright © David Bedford 2002
Illustrations copyright © Mandy Stanley 2002
David Bedford and Mandy Stanley have asserted their rights
to be identified as the author and illustrator of this work under
the Copyright, Designs and Patents Act, 1988
All rights reserved • ISBN 978-1-84895-199-0
Printed in China • LTP/1800/0151/0910
2 4 6 8 10 9 7 5 3 1

# The Healthy Wolf

David Bedford

Illustrated by Mandy Stanley

LITTLE TIGER PRESS

Wilfred was a greedy young wolf who liked
all the wrong foods . . .
Tangy, crunchy smoky-bacon potato chips.

Mm! Mmmmmm!

Sweet, chewy chocolate bars.

Aaahh!

All washed down with lots of sugary, fizzy pop.

Yum!

But there was one very naughty food that Wilfred wanted to eat more than anything. Juicy, tasty . . .

# CHILDREN!

But he never did. After years of
eating chips and chocolate bars,
Wilfred was very unhealthy, and
much too slow to catch any.

Tee-hee!

As the years went by Wilfred
grew more and more unhealthy.

It got so bad that his teeth were
too rotten to chew anything.

By the time he was ten the only food he could eat was icky sticky porridge! Yuk! Then one day, his diet changed forever . . .

The Brownbread family all thought
Wilfred looked hilarious when they first met him.
"Look at that silly old wolf with porridge on his chin,"
laughed Sarah. "He couldn't scare a flea!"

But Mrs. Brownbread felt a bit sorry for him.
"Don't laugh," she said. "Let's take him home
with us and make him better."

Fortunately, Mr. Brownbread was a dentist, so Wilfred got his teeth fixed for free. Unfortunately, they were all rotten and needed pulling out!

Then he gave Wilfred new fangs made out of hard plastic. "From now on you must brush your teeth three times a day, and eat plenty of fresh fruit. Look at me, I'm full of fruit," said Mr. Brownbread.

"Then you must be very good for my teeth!" said Wilfred, as he lunged to gobble up Mr. Brownbread.

SNAP!
SNAP!
SNAP!

But Mr. Brownbread
was too quick. He was up an
apple tree, raining apples
down on Wilfred before he
could so much as sniff at him!

Next Wilfred went to see
Mrs. Brownbread . . .

As a doctor she was horrified when she saw what he'd been eating all these years!
"You are extremely unhealthy, and from now on you must only eat good foods, like me. I'm full of good foods."

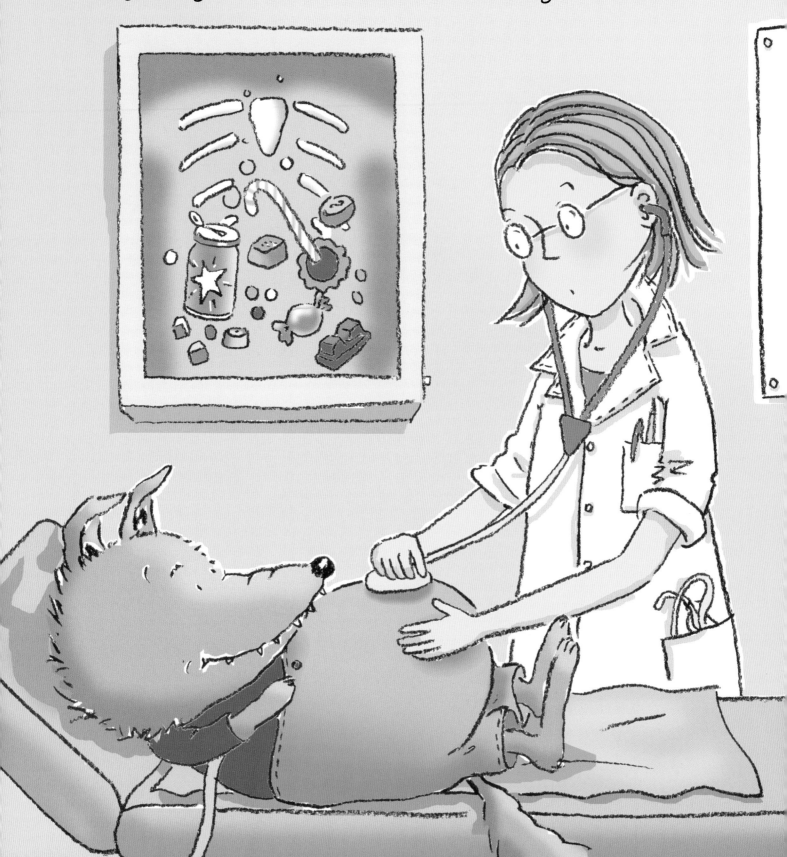

"Okay, then!" said Wilfred, "If that's what the doctor has ordered." And he lunged to gobble up Mrs. Brownbread.

# SNAP! SNAP!

But Mrs. Brownbread was too quick.
She hid in a closet before he
could take one bite!

Upstairs, Sarah was getting ready to go running.

"Would you like to come running with me?" asked Sarah.
"If you run every day you'll soon be fit and healthy like
the rest of us."
"No thanks!" said Wilfred, "I'm not allowed fast food,
so you'd better stay right where you are!"
And he lunged straight for her . . .

Unfortunately, she was very good at running.

"You're even sillier than you look," she laughed.

Wilfred was fed up that everyone else was too quick for him. He was determined to catch them. Every day for a whole week he ate . . .

Apples for breakfast.

Mm! Mmmmm!

Bananas for lunch.

Aaahh!

And soup for dinner.

Yum!

After each meal he brushed his fangs
until the sharp points sparkled.

And every day he went out running with Sarah.

Each day, he got nearer . . .

and nearer . . .

and **nearer,**

Until...

he ran right past her!

He'd had so much fun that
week that he'd forgotten all about
eating her, and just wanted to beat her!

Three cheers for Wilfred, the healthy wolf!